Use your 3-D glasses when you view this book.

3D-INATOR

Based on the episode "Picture This"
Based on the series created by Dan Povenmire and Jeff "Swampy" Marsh
Story adapted by Michael Teitelbaum

Reader's Digest Children's Books®

New York, New York • Montréal, Québec • Bath, United Kingdom

Phineas and Ferb had just turned their garage upside down—literally.

"Why on earth would you do that?" their father asked.

"We're searching for Ferb's favorite skateboard," Phineas explained.

"Does it have a Union Jack on it?" their dad asked.

"That's the one!" Phineas exclaimed.

"Turn the garage right-side up and come in the house. I've solved your mystery," their father said. He then showed the boys photos of their grandfather riding Ferb's skateboard in England.

"Ferb, you must have left your skateboard in England the last time we were there," Phineas said. "I know! We'll create a highly intricate machine that will transport any object from anywhere on the globe to our backyard!"

"Why don't you just build a new skateboard?" their father asked.

Phineas stared at his dad as if he had just suggested the strangest thing in the world.

"If it's all the same with you, Father, we're going to build the machine," Ferb told him.

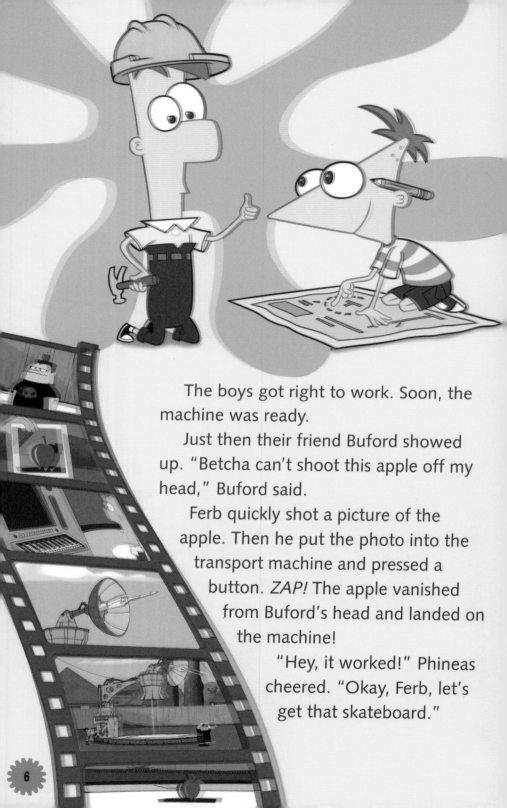

The boys got right to work. Soon, the machine was ready.

Just then their friend Buford showed up. "Betcha can't shoot this apple off my head," Buford said.

Ferb quickly shot a picture of the apple. Then he put the photo into the transport machine and pressed a button. *ZAP!* The apple vanished from Buford's head and landed on the machine!

"Hey, it worked!" Phineas cheered. "Okay, Ferb, let's get that skateboard."

Ferb used the picture of his grandfather on the skateboard to transport it back from England. Unfortunately, they transported their grandfather's feet along *with* the skateboard. Phineas and Ferb quickly returned their grandpa's feet, although they ended up going on backwards.

"Now, let's try out that half-pipe," Phineas said. Then, looking around, he added, "Hey, where's Perry?" he asked. His pet platypus had gone missing.

In his guise as Agent P, Phineas and Ferb's mild-mannered pet, Perry the Platypus, entered his secret lair for a briefing from Major Monogram.

"Hello, Agent P," Major Monogram began. "We have recently discovered that all of the mimes in Danville Park have been trapped in actual invisible boxes. It took days to discover because, well, everyone just assumed they were really good mimes."

Agent P watched videos of mimes struggling to get free from invisible boxes.

Major Monogram continued. "We're convinced that it has something to do with the machine Dr. Doofenshmirtz has been working on. We're sending you a photo of his new -inator. It looks evil all right. You'd better destroy it. Good luck, Agent P."

Agent P set off to find Dr. Doofenshmirtz's latest -inator.

Meanwhile in the backyard, Phineas and Ferb's friend Isabella joined the group. "Hey guys, whatcha doin'?" she asked.

"We're conducting an experiment with our mega-half-pipe and our new photo-transporter," Phineas explained. "Okay, Ferb, let her rip."

Ferb rocketed down the huge half-pipe at blazing speed. He whipped around the bottom then shot back up, zooming high into the sky. As Ferb began to plunge toward the ground, Phineas fed his picture into the transport machine and…

ZAP!

…Ferb instantly vanished, reappearing on the machine's platform. A moment later, Ferb's skateboard landed in his hands.

Their sister Candace saw the whole thing from her bedroom window. "I've got to tell Mom. Where did she say she was going again?"

Then she remembered that her mother was going to a cultural festival with Isabella's mom. Candace quickly headed to the festival.

Across town, Agent P had just burst into Dr. Doofenshmirtz's headquarters.

"Perry the Platypus. Oh, big surprise," Dr. Doofenshmirtz said. He pulled out a remote control and pressed a button."By the way, you're trapped in an invisible box." Agent P tried to escape, but he ran into invisible walls. He was indeed trapped inside!

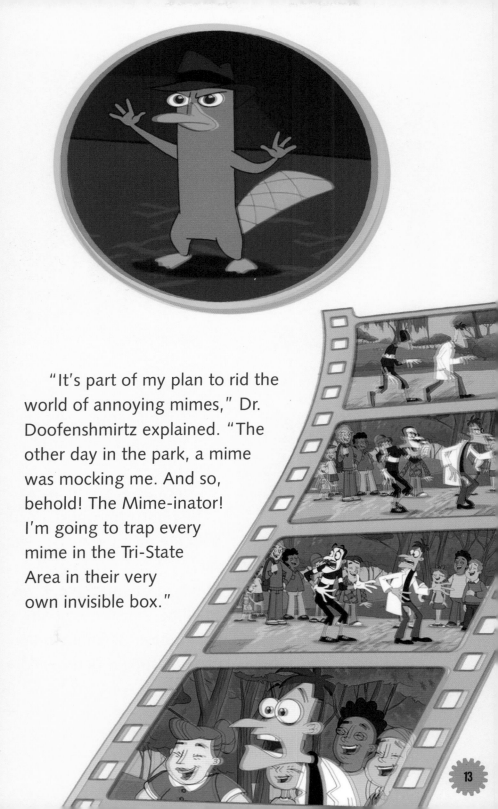

"It's part of my plan to rid the world of annoying mimes," Dr. Doofenshmirtz explained. "The other day in the park, a mime was mocking me. And so, behold! The Mime-inator! I'm going to trap every mime in the Tri-State Area in their very own invisible box."

At the festival, Candace had just had her picture taken.

That gave her an idea. "The photo-transporter can help me bust the boys," she said. "I'll put my Mom's photo in the machine, then she'll be transported right to the boys! Their invention can't disappear before Mom

sees it, because she'll be in it! It's foolproof. Phineas and Ferb will be busted once and for all."

Candace borrowed the photographer's camera, found her mom at the festival, and snapped her picture. Then she raced home.

Back at his headquarters, Dr. Doofenshmirtz
worked on the next phase of his evil plan. "My
Mime-inator worked so well with the mimes, I've
decided to put everyone in the Tri-State Area in an
invisible box," he told Agent P, who was still trapped.
As Dr. Doofenshmirtz wheeled his machine to the
roof of the building, Agent P cleverly used his power
glass cutter to break out of the box. He tackled Dr.
Doofenshmirtz, and reached out to push the self-
destruct button on the machine.

Dr. Doofenshmirtz cried out, "No, Perry the Platypus, don't push the…"

In the backyard, Phineas had realized Perry hadn't come home. "I know," Phineas said, "we'll put a photo of Perry into the transport device."

Suddenly, Agent P vanished from the rooftop, and reappeared as Perry the Platypus in the backyard.

Just then, Candace ran up to the transport machine carrying her mom's photo. "You're so busted!" she shouted. She stuck her mom's picture into the machine and pressed the button.

Meanwhile, Candace's mom was still at the festival. She was blindfolded, swinging a

stick, trying to hit a piñata. She took several swings, then the transporter beam engulfed her in a green glow. She suddenly vanished, mid-swing!

She reappeared in the backyard, still blindfolded, swinging wildly, thinking she was still at the festival.

"Yes, yes, it worked!" Candace cried. "Mom, look!"

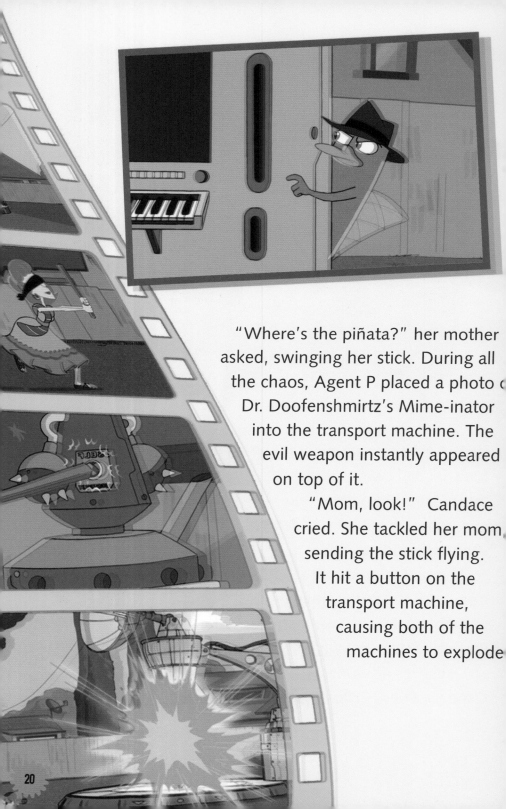

"Where's the piñata?" her mother asked, swinging her stick. During all the chaos, Agent P placed a photo o Dr. Doofenshmirtz's Mime-inator into the transport machine. The evil weapon instantly appeared on top of it.

"Mom, look!" Candace cried. She tackled her mom, sending the stick flying. It hit a button on the transport machine, causing both of the machines to explode

Candace's mom pulled off her blindfold and saw nothing but Phineas and Ferb and their friends in the backyard.

"Oh, my goodness. I walked all the way home?" she asked, realizing that she was no longer at the festival, but back home. "I guess it's hard to judge distances blindfolded. Well, snacks, anyone?"

"B-B-B-B-But," Candace stammered in disbelief. Her plan to bust her brothers was foiled once again!

Ferb got his favorite skateboard back, but the photo-transporter was totally destroyed.

"Can't you just build it again?" asked Buford.

"Where would the fun it that be?" said Phineas.

Just then he noticed his pet platypus had returned.

"Hey, look, Perry's back!" he said.

Ferb led everyone inside for a snack. It was a good day.